MW01643619

WARRIORS OF HISTORY

British Redcoats

by Ann Weil

Consultant:
Professor Julie Taddeo
Department of History
University of Maryland
College Park, Maryland

Mankato, Minnesota

Edge Books are published by Capstone Press,
151 Good Counsel Drive, P.O. Box 669, Mankato, Minnesota 56002.
www.capstonepress.com

Copyright © 2008 by Capstone Press, a Capstone Publishers company.
All rights reserved. No part of this publication may be reproduced in whole or in part, or stored in a retrieval system, or transmitted in any form or by any means, electronic, mechanical, photocopying, recording, or otherwise, without written permission of the publisher.
For information regarding permission, write to Capstone Press,
151 Good Counsel Drive, P.O. Box 669, Dept. R, Mankato, Minnesota 56002.
Printed in the United States of America

Library of Congress Cataloging-in-Publication Data
Weil, Ann.
British redcoats / by Ann Weil.
p. cm. — (Edge books. Warriors of history)
Includes bibliographical references and index.
ISBN-13: 978-1-4296-1310-1 (hardcover)
ISBN-10: 1-4296-1310-6 (hardcover)
1. Great Britain. Army — History — Juvenile literature. I. Title. II. Series.
UA649.W45 2008
355.00941'09033 — dc22 2007029958

Summary: Describes the life of a British soldier in the 1700s, including his training and weapons.

Editorial Credits
Mandy Robbins, editor; Thomas Emery, set designer; Kyle Grenz, book designer; Jo Miller, photo researcher; Tod Smith, illustrator; Krista Ward, colorist

Photo Credits
Alamy/Classic Image, 6; North Wind Picture Archives, 23; The Print Collector, 26–27
Art Resource, N.Y./HIP/Oxford Science Archive, Oxford, Great Britian, 10–11
Corbis/Fine Art Photographic Library, 8–9
Getty Images Inc./Hulton Archive, 24–25
James P. Rowan, cover, 28–29
Mary Evans Picture Library, 4, 12–13, 14, 17; Douglas McCarthy, 18–19

1 2 3 4 5 6 13 12 11 10 09 08

TABLE OF CONTENTS

CHAPTER 1

the British Empire

LEARN ABOUT:

- A large empire
- British soldiers
- Recruiting

Officers rode horses during training and battle, while most infantry soldiers traveled on foot.

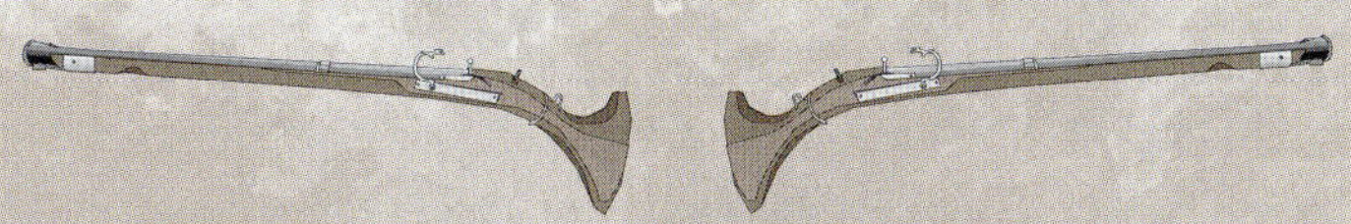

In the 1700s, the British Empire was growing. Britain had colonies in North and South America, Asia, and Australia. These colonies made up the British Empire. The king of England sent British soldiers to guard these new colonies. It took weeks or months at sea to reach some of them. Most new soldiers had never traveled farther than they could walk from home.

Many of these soldiers were young men who had little reason to stay in England. They were not married. They had no jobs and no money. The army gave them food and clothes.

The term "Redcoat" did not become the popular slang term for a British soldier until the late 1800s. In the 1700s, they were known as "Regulars" or "The King's Men." Regulars were infantrymen. They marched into battle on foot.

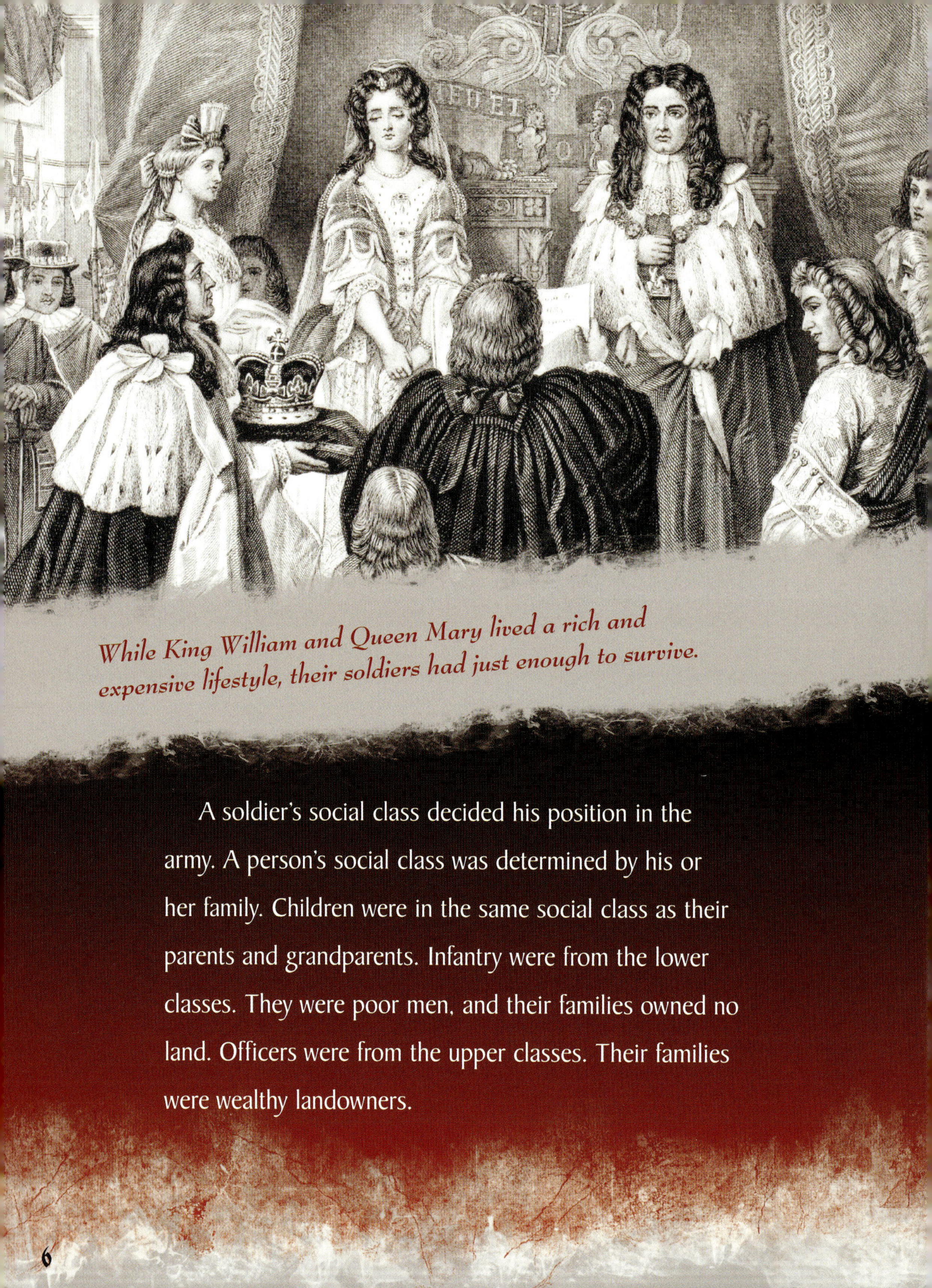

While King William and Queen Mary lived a rich and expensive lifestyle, their soldiers had just enough to survive.

A soldier's social class decided his position in the army. A person's social class was determined by his or her family. Children were in the same social class as their parents and grandparents. Infantry were from the lower classes. They were poor men, and their families owned no land. Officers were from the upper classes. Their families were wealthy landowners.

A VOLUNTEER ARMY

All soldiers in the British Army were volunteers. But it was rarely their first choice for a way of life. Some volunteers worked on farms. After a harvest, there was less work. Sometimes, a bad harvest might leave families hungry. Out-of-work men had very few choices. They knew that life in the British Army was tough. But starving at home was worse.

When a man agreed to join the British Army, he took a shilling from the recruiting officer. This coin sealed the deal. It was enough money to buy a good dinner to celebrate his new life in the army. When a recruit took the shilling, he signed on for life.

Edge Fact

During wartime, the army needed soldiers to replace those who were killed or wounded. Some criminals were given the choice between going to jail or joining the army.

THE INDUSTRIAL REVOLUTION

The Industrial Revolution began in England in the mid-1700s. Before that time, lower-class men had more options than to join the army. They farmed land owned by wealthy upper-class people. Some lower-class families spun wool or did other work from home.

Lower-class families rented farmland and gave a part of their crop to the wealthy landowners as payment.

The Industrial Revolution changed the landscape of Great Britain. Smoke stacks towered over towns that were once farming villages.

During the Industrial Revolution, inventions changed the old way of life. Spinning machines made thread faster than people could using a spinning wheel. New machines like the iron rolling mill changed the iron and steel industries too.

Many people moved to cities to work in factories. But some men couldn't adapt to factory work. They chose to join the army.

CHAPTER II

Life as a Soldier

LEARN ABOUT:

- *Basic training*
- *British officers*
- *Flogging*

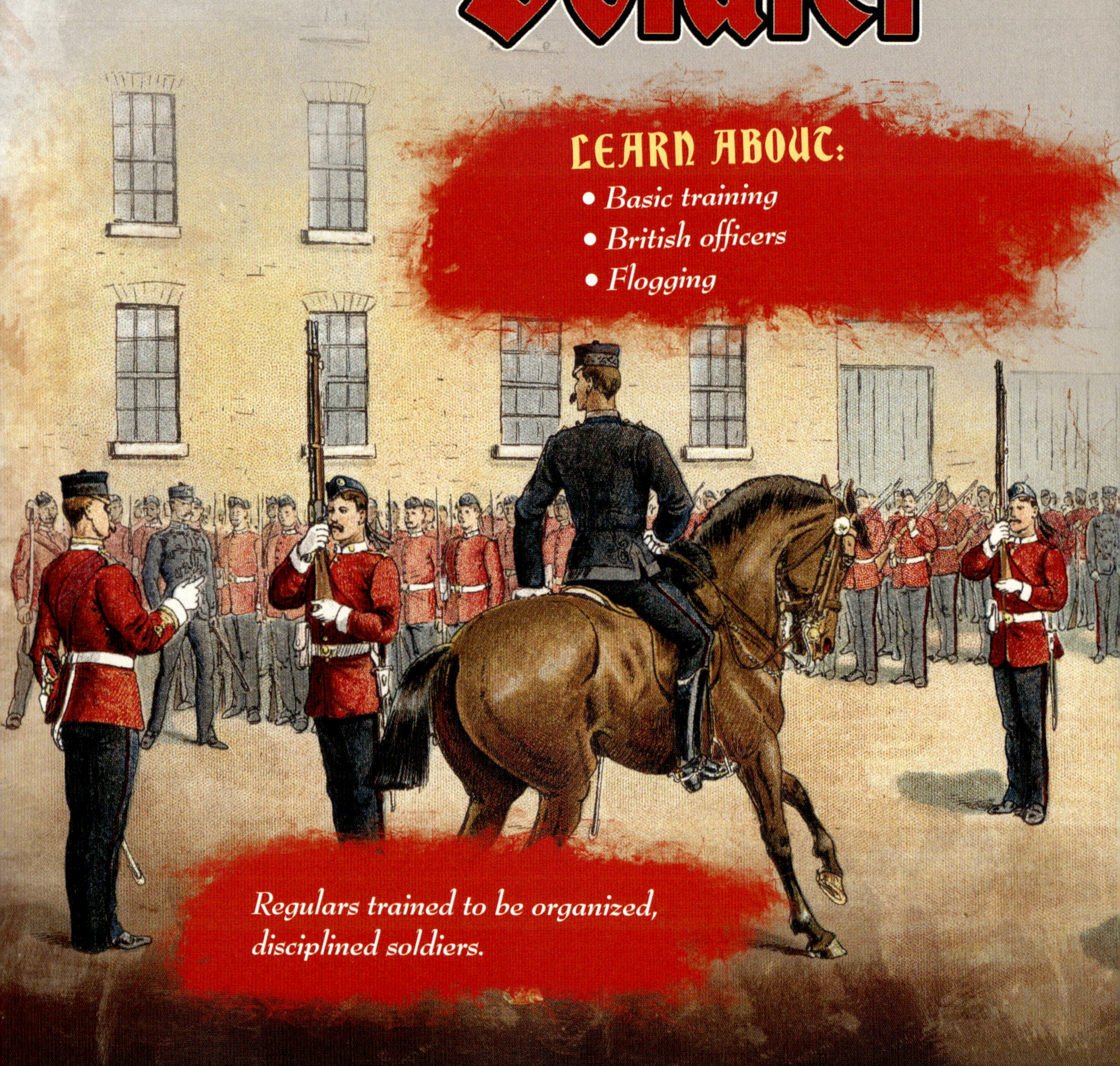

Regulars trained to be organized, disciplined soldiers.

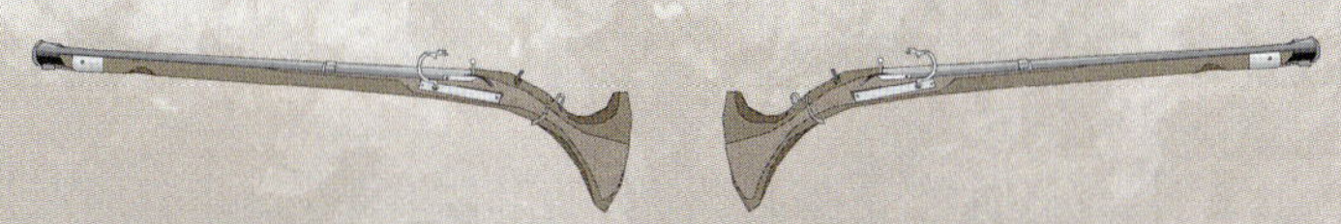

The British Army fought in a very structured way. It took a year or more of basic training to turn a new recruit into an able soldier. Regulars trained every day. They learned to line up shoulder-to-shoulder and march together in step. Regulars also mastered their weapons. Soldiers learned to fire and quickly reload muskets. They also learned to use long, sharp spikes called bayonets. These weapons were attached to their muskets. Regulars did not fire their muskets during a bayonet charge. Instead, they stabbed enemies to death.

A few soldiers rose through the ranks to become officers. But most British officers came from wealthy families. These men weren't the firstborn sons, so they wouldn't inherit any of the family's wealth. They turned to the army to earn a living.

A British officer did not have to train for his position. Instead, some officers read books about how to win battles. A few officers were good leaders. Many were not.

Soldiers who lived in army barracks had to be very neat. Officers inspected their stations every day.

Most soldiers in England lived in private houses. The houses were crowded and had few comforts. Still, the houses were better than the damp, dirty shacks where many of the soldiers' relatives lived.

Some soldiers lived in barracks at an army camp. Barracks were crowded too. A room that was only 18 by 36 feet (5.5 by 11 meters) might house as many as 19 soldiers. This was where they slept, ate, and relaxed off-duty.

Regulars were given a straw mattress, a blanket, and sheets. They slept on folding beds and stored their belongings in a box.

A soldier's day began before dawn. Drum beats woke him. He folded his bed, washed, and got dressed. Then he ate breakfast in his barracks. After breakfast, officers inspected each soldier and his bunk area to make sure they met the army's standards. After morning inspection, Regulars had duties. Some were on guard duty. Some made musket cartridges. Some jobs, like cleaning the toilets, were used as punishments for bad behavior.

A bugle call at noon told the soldiers that it was time for dinner. In the afternoon, soldiers were kept busy with drills and training. Another bugle call announced supper time. After supper, there were more duties and free time until after sunset. Soldiers then returned to their barracks to sleep.

Edge Fact

Regulars did more than train and fight. They also cleaned and repaired their own clothes and gear.

FLOGGING

The British Army used harsh ways to control soldiers. The most serious crimes, such as murder or deserting the army, were punished by death. Other crimes, such as being late for duty, missing drill, or stealing, were punished by flogging.

When a soldier was flogged, he had to strip to the waist. Then, an army drummer whipped him on his bare back. The number of lashes depended on what the soldier had done. Someone who committed a small crime might receive 25 lashes. The maximum was 1,000 lashes. These lashes would be spread out over days or weeks.

Flogging was horribly painful. The whip ripped off skin. The bloody wounds took weeks to heal.

Edge Fact

During the American Revolution, the Americans called the Regulars "bloody backs." This nickname came from the British practice of flogging soldiers.

Most Regulars were quick to obey the rules. They didn't want to risk the horrible pain of flogging.

Redcoats in Battle

LEARN ABOUT:

- *Gear and weapons*
- *The American Revolution*
- *War wounds and disease*

British soldiers charged into battle in long straight rows.

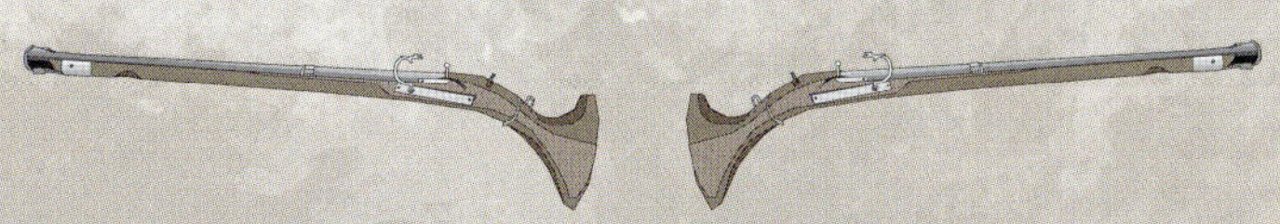

The British Army was organized into regiments. A colonel owned the regiment. The king of England paid colonels for the use of their soldiers. Some colonels fought alongside their troops. Other colonels chose the safety of their homes over the battlefield.

Each regiment had 10 companies of about 40 soldiers. Eight companies were Regulars. Two were flank companies. The flank companies were grenadiers and light infantry. Their main job was to protect the Regulars from a side attack. Grenadiers attacked enemies by throwing small bombs called grenades. Light infantry distracted the enemy with small attacks on foot.

The tallest and strongest soldiers were grenadiers. They could throw grenades the farthest. Grenades were hollow iron balls filled with black powder. The grenadier lit the wick and threw it. When the burning wick reached the powder, the grenade exploded.

Hat
Regulars wore many different types of hats throughout history. Most Regulars wore the three-sided hat during the American Revolution.
Musket
In the 1700s, most Regulars used the Brown Bess flintlock musket.
Sword
Regulars used swords in hand-to-hand combat.
Red jacket
All regiments wore red jackets. But the style and decoration on the jackets were unique to each group.

MASTERING MUSKETS

A Regular's main weapon was a musket. Muskets had a short range. Regulars had to be less than 240 feet (73 meters) from enemy soldiers to hit them. During battle, Regulars marched in lines, shoulder-to-shoulder. Once they got close enough to the enemy, they fired.

Regulars trained so they could fire and reload their muskets quickly. Still, reloading took more than a minute. Because of the length of the guns, soldiers had to reload standing up. Some Regulars in line fired while others reloaded. Their bright red jackets made it easy to see who was reloading and needed cover.

Edge Fact

According to myth, British soldiers wore red to hide the bloodstains on their clothes. But the real reason had to do with money. At that time, red dye cost less than other dyes.

THE AMERICAN REVOLUTION

Great Britain ruled many colonies in North America in the mid-1700s. Many people in 13 of these colonies resented being controlled by a government an ocean away. They wanted to have a say in making their laws. After several conflicts between the British and the colonists, the American Revolution (1775–1783) began.

The colonists didn't fight like European soldiers. Most were not soldiers at all. They were farmers and tradesmen who were not trained to fight. They couldn't always win in a battle, so they targeted British officers. Some American rebels hid in the woods with rifles. They waited for the British to march by. Then they opened fire on the British officers.

British soldiers were not trained for this sneaky type of warfare. Even their uniforms worked against them. The bright red color was helpful in battles where it was hard to see your fellow soldiers. But during the American Revolution, the red jackets were like a target on their backs. In the end, the Americans beat the British and won independence.

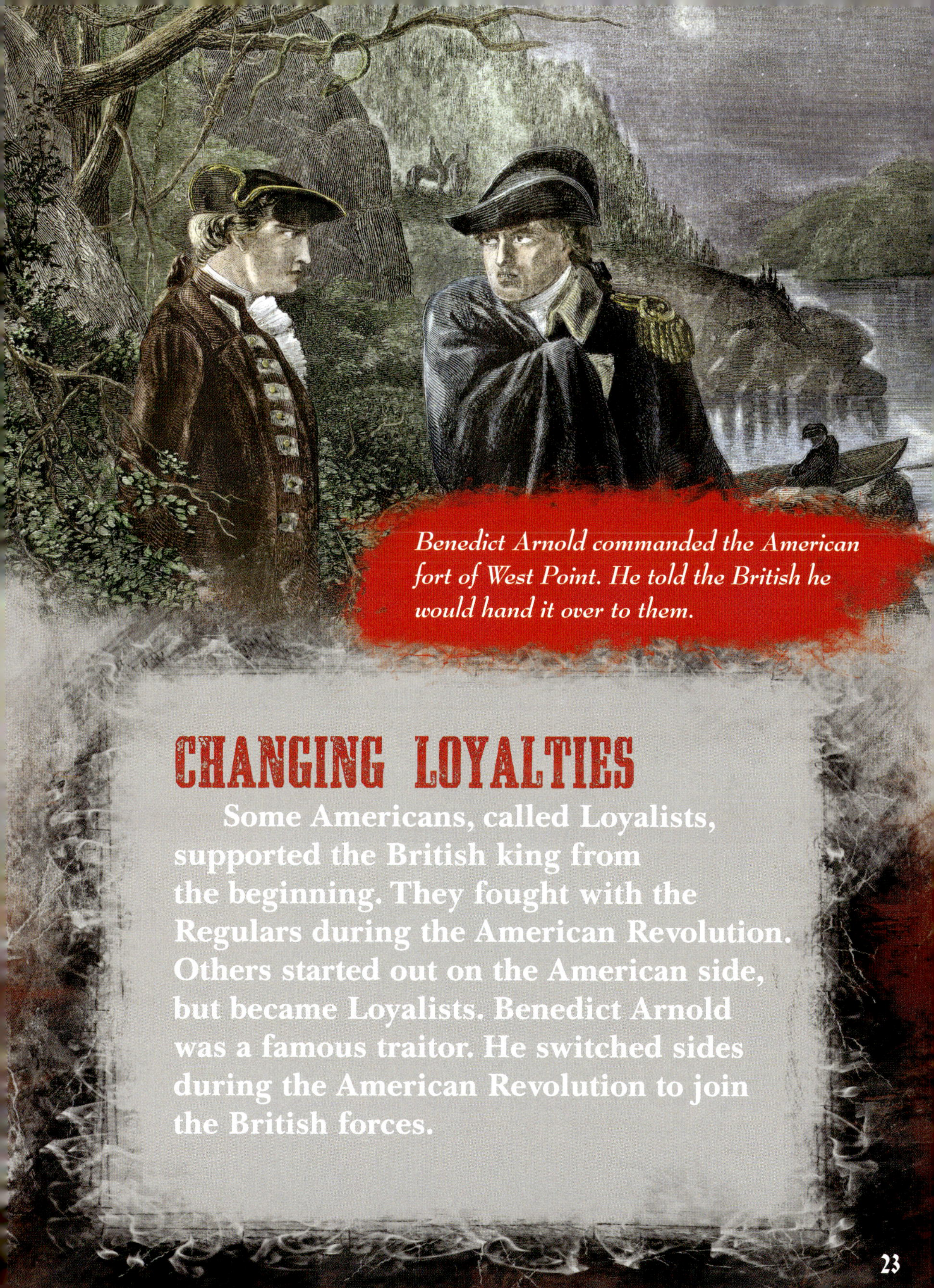

Benedict Arnold commanded the American fort of West Point. He told the British he would hand it over to them.

CHANGING LOYALTIES

Some Americans, called Loyalists, supported the British king from the beginning. They fought with the Regulars during the American Revolution. Others started out on the American side, but became Loyalists. Benedict Arnold was a famous traitor. He switched sides during the American Revolution to join the British forces.

In every war, British soldiers suffered horrible wounds. Bullets and shells tore through flesh. Cannonballs ripped off legs and arms. Many soldiers died on the battlefield. Wounded soldiers were treated at field hospitals. These hospitals were dirty and crowded. Doctors amputated limbs without putting the patient to sleep or numbing the pain. Many soldiers died from shock or infection at field hospitals.

Wounded soldiers often lay on the battlefield for hours before they could be brought to field hospitals.

In America, diseases were even more deadly to British soldiers than cannonballs and bullets. More soldiers died from disease than war wounds. Poor diets and crowded living sped the spread of disease.

CHAPTER IV

Changing Colors

LEARN ABOUT:

- *Khaki uniforms*
- *The Battle of Isandlwana*
- *British soldiers today*

The British were overwhelmingly defeated by the Zulus during the Battle of Isandlwana Hill.

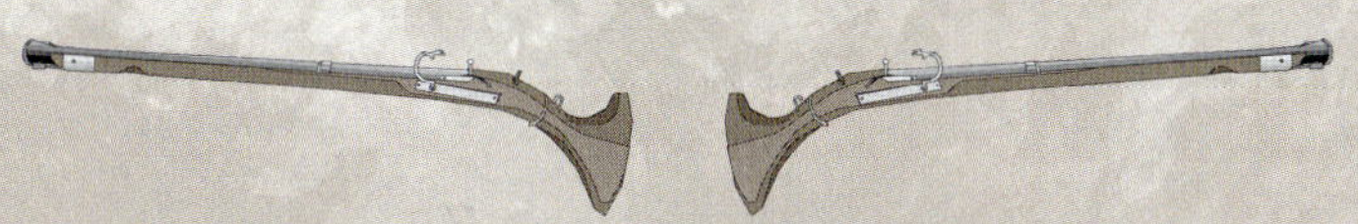

In 1848, Sir Harry Burnett Lumsden introduced a new uniform for British soldiers in India. The new uniform was made of cotton dyed the color of dust. The new uniform was called khaki, from the Indian word for dust or ashes. Khaki uniforms were more practical than the traditional red jackets. Over the years, khaki began to replace red as the official color for British Army uniforms.

In 1879, British soldiers fought Zulu warriors at the Battle of Isandlwana Hill in Africa. The British made the mistake of wearing the old red jackets during this battle. The British officers expected an easy victory against the Zulus. But the British soldiers were outnumbered, and their red uniforms made them easy targets. Fierce Zulu warriors armed with stabbing spears surrounded the British. After a brutal hand-to-hand battle, the Zulus won. Only a few British soldiers survived.

The British Army dressed its soldiers in khaki uniforms in World War I (1914–1918). By then, warfare styles had changed. Instead of fighting in straight lines, soldiers hid in trenches and shot from great distances. Red jackets would have been easy targets for enemies with high-powered rifles.

Today, British soldiers are stationed all over the world, as they were in colonial days. They keep peace and protect people in many nations. Their uniforms are no longer red, but they are still a brave, strong fighting force.

A few British Army units wear the traditional red uniform on special occasions.

Glossary

amputate (AM-pyuh-tayt) — to cut off an arm, leg, or other body part, usually because the part is damaged

barracks (BAYR-uhks) — the part of a fort where soldiers sleep

bayonet (BAY-uh-net) — a long metal blade attached to the end of a rifle or musket

colony (KAH-luh-nee) — land governed by another country; a group of people who leave their own country to settle in a colony are called colonists.

empire (EM-pire) — a group of countries that have the same ruler

grenade (gruh-NADE) — a small bomb that can be thrown or launched

infantry (IN-fuhn-tree) — soldiers trained to fight and travel on foot

musket (MUHSS-kit) — a gun with a long barrel that was used before the rifle was invented

Read More

Allen, Thomas B. *Remember Valley Forge: Patriots, Tories, and Redcoats Tell Their Stories.* The Remember Series. Washington, D.C.: National Geographic, 2007.

Burgan, Michael. *Benedict Arnold: American Hero and Traitor.* Graphic Biographies. Mankato, Minn.: Capstone Press, 2007.

Gordon, Sharon. *Great Britain.* Discovering Cultures. New York: Benchmark Books, 2004.

Internet Sites

FactHound offers a safe, fun way to find Internet sites related to this book. All of the sites on FactHound have been researched by our staff.

Here's how:

1. Visit *www.facthound.com*
2. Choose your grade level.
3. Type in this book ID **1429613106** for age-appropriate sites. You may also browse subjects by clicking on letters, or by clicking on pictures and words.
4. Click on the **Fetch It** button.

FactHound will fetch the best sites for you!

Index